With Chord Symbols for Guitar and Keyboard Accompaniments.
Arranged by JOHN ROBERT BROWN

The clarinet has always been at the forefront of jazz music. During the Swing era, it was the virtuoso clarinettists, such as Benny Goodman, Artie Shaw and Woody Herman who rose to great fame.

Later, during the revival of traditional jazz, the clarinet was again to the fore on many of the 'trad' hit records.

This book contains tunes that were associated with jazz and the clarinet, arranged to give the flavour of jazz improvisation.

To play the pieces idiomatically, dotted quaver — semi-quaver figures (♪) should be played with a twelve-eight feel (♩♪). It is appropriate to use vibrato on all long notes.

JOHN ROBERT BROWN

First Published 1985
© International Music Publications

 International Music Publications
Southend Road, Woodford Green, Essex IG8 8HN, England.

1-2-51034

Begin The Beguine

Words & Music by
COLE PORTER

4

Body And Soul

Words by ROBERT SOUR,
EDWARD HEYMAN
and FRANK EYTON
Music by JOHN GREEN

I'm Gonna Sit Right Down
And Write Myself A Letter

Words by JOE YOUNG
Music by FRED E. AHLERT

Memory Lane Music Ltd, 11 Great Marlborough Street, London W1/Anglo Pic Music Co Ltd, 22 Denmark Street, London W1/
Bucks Music, 19-20 Poland Street, London W1

Won't You Come Home Bill Bailey?

Words and Music by
HUGHIE CANNON

Dancing In The Dark

Words by HOWARD DIETZ
Music by ARTHUR SCHWARTZ

Hello Dolly

Words and Music by
JERRY HERMAN

I Got Rhythm

Words by IRA GERSHWIN
Music by GEORGE GERSHWIN

Is It True What They Say About Dixie?

Words by IRVING CAESAR,
SAMMY LERNER & GERALD MARKS

I Want To Be Happy

Words by IRVING CAESAR
Music by VINCENT YOUMANS

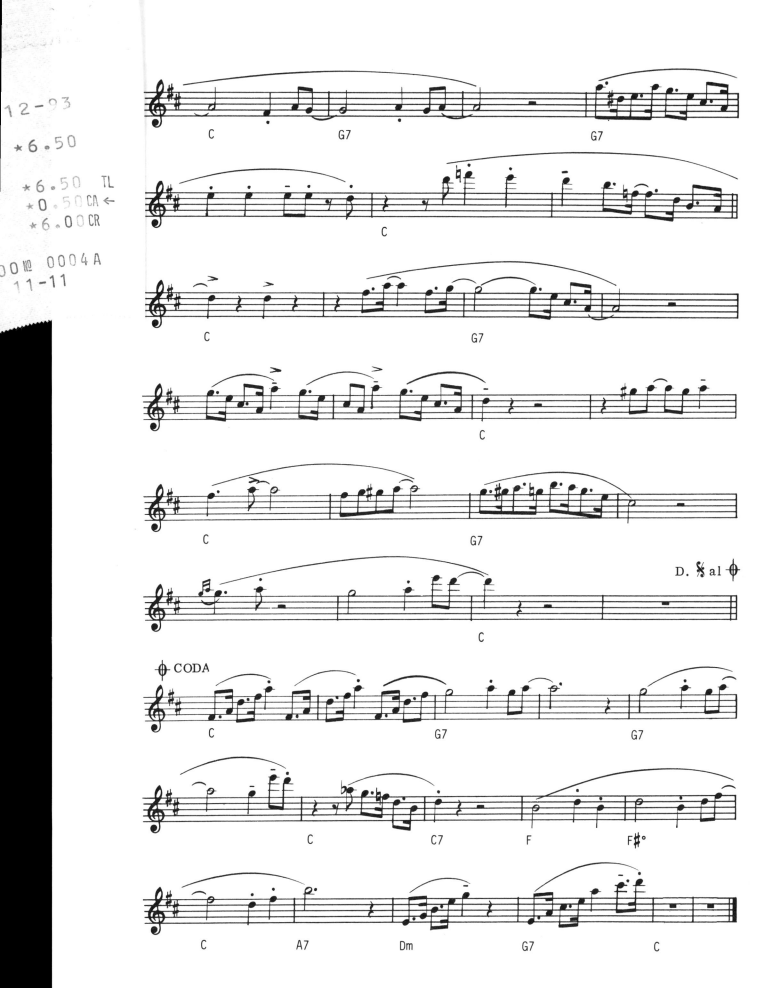

Limehouse Blues

Words by DOUGLAS FURBER
Music by PHILIP BRAHAM

My Heart Stood Still

Words by LORENZ HART
Music by RICHARD RODGERS

Liza

Words by GUS KAHN
and IRA GERSHWIN
Music by GEORGE GERSHWIN

Nobody Knows The Trouble I've Seen

TRADITIONAL
Arranged by
JOHN ROBERT BROWN

Love Is Just Around The Corner

Words & Music by
LEO ROBIN &
LEWIS E. GENSLER

Swing Low Sweet Chariot

arr. JOHN ROBERT BROWN
TRADITIONAL

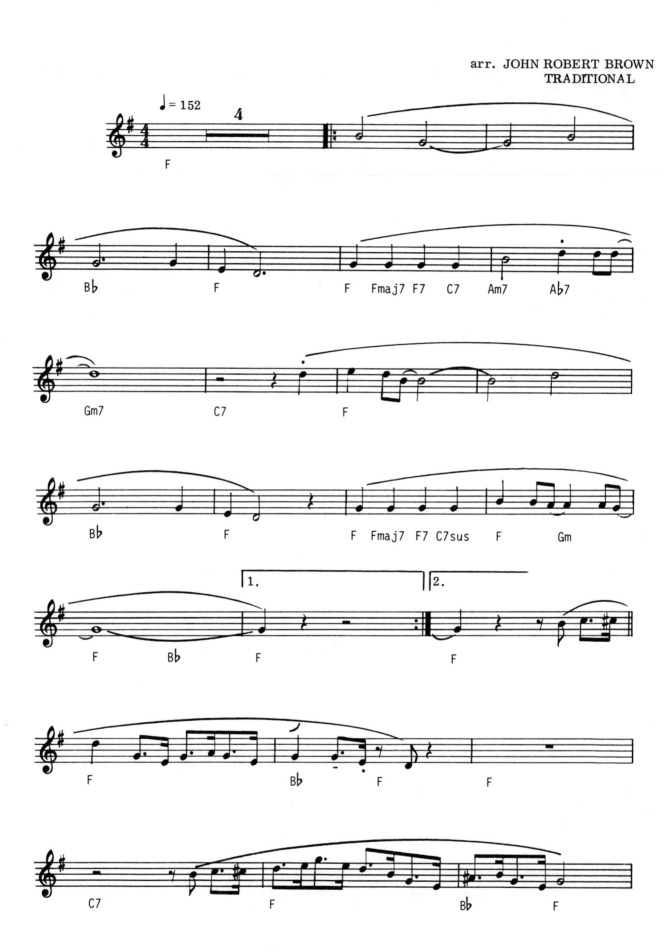

A Taste Of Honey

Words by RIC MARLOW
Music by BOBBY SCOTT

The World Is Waiting For The Sunrise

Music by ERNEST SEITZ
Words by EUGENE LOCKHART

You Took Advantage Of Me

Words by LORENZ HART
Music by RICHARD RODGERS

Yesterdays

Words by OTTO HARBACH
Music by JEROME KERN

Panama

By
WILLIAM H. TYERS